Goldilocks

DOM DeLUISE

Goldilocks

ILLUSTRATED BY
CHRISTOPHER SANTORO

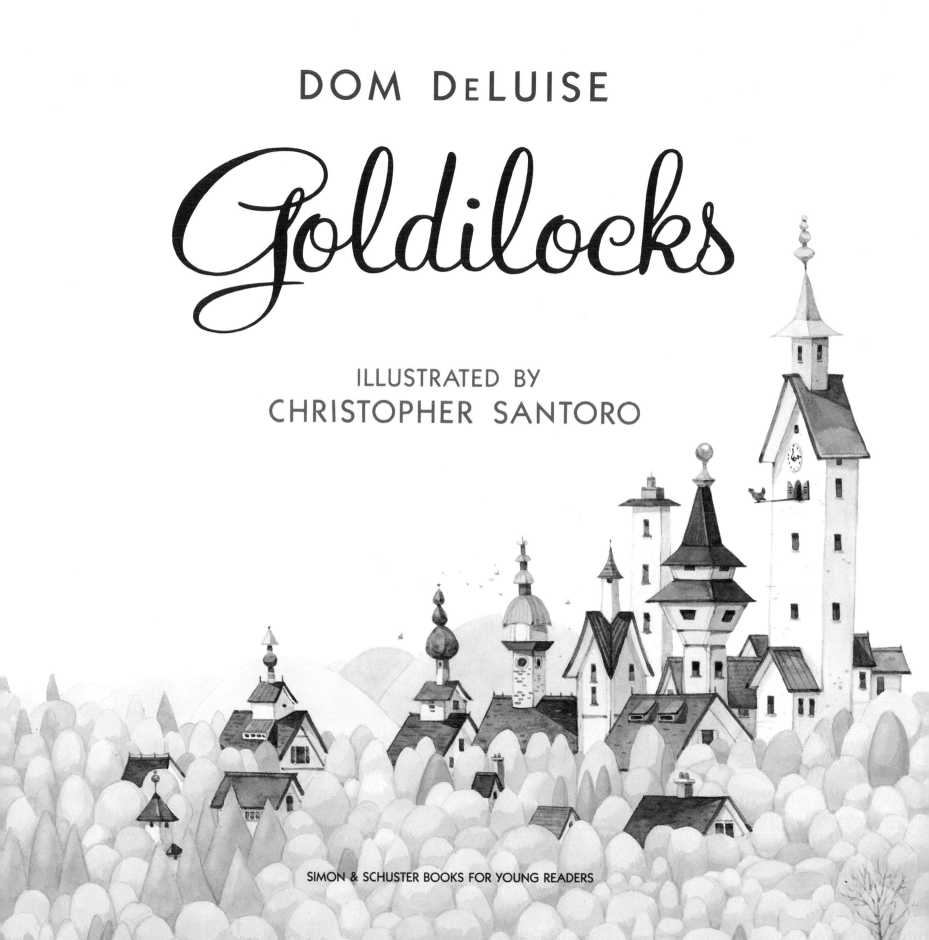

SIMON & SCHUSTER BOOKS FOR YOUNG READERS

SIMON & SCHUSTER BOOKS FOR YOUNG READERS
An imprint of Simon & Schuster Children's Publishing Division
1230 Avenue of the Americas, New York, New York 10020
Text copyright © 1992 by Petmida Incorporated
Illustrations copyright © 1992 by Christopher Santoro
All rights reserved including the right of
reproduction in whole or in part in any form.
SIMON & SCHUSTER BOOKS FOR YOUNG READERS
is a trademark of Simon & Schuster.
Designed by Vicki Kalajian
The text of this book is set in 15 pt. Esprit Book.
The illustrations were done in watercolor.
Printed and bound in the United States of America.

10 9 8 7 6 5 4 3

Library of Congress Cataloging-in-Publication Data
DeLuise, Dom. Goldilocks / by Dom DeLuise : illustrated by
Christopher Santoro. p. cm. Summary: The well-known comedian
presents his own rendition of the folktale with a slightly different twist
at the end. [1. Folklore. 2. Bears – Folklore.] I. Santoro, Christopher,
ill. II. Title. PZ8.1.D3795Go 1992 398.2–dc20 [E] 91-20213 CIP
ISBN: 0-671-74690-1

To Carol, my mama bear, with love.
Thanks for *bearing* with me
all these years.
—D.D.

To Jamie.
—C.S.

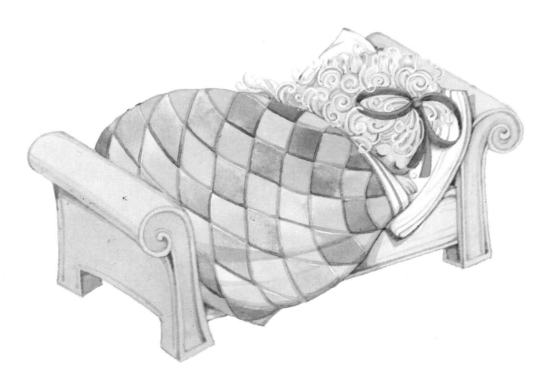

Once upon a time, in a forest far away, lived a beautiful little girl with the most gorgeous blond hair you ever saw. It was very long, very shiny, and very curly. I mean it really got your attention.

In the forest, if you were a very, very tall man—why, they would call you The Giant—figures! And if you snarled at people all the time, they would call you Grumpy—makes sense! So it was only natural that this beautiful girl with gorgeous, long, blond, shiny, curly hair should be called Goldilocks. She must have had a real name long ago, but this story is so old that no one remembers it. Everybody just knew her as Goldilocks.

Goldilocks had such beautiful hair,
people were always complimenting her
on how wonderful she looked and pretty
soon she began to think so, too. And
that's when her troubles really began.

Her mother and father would say, "Goldilocks, you cannot go out and play until you have finished all your homework," but because Goldilocks was so spoiled and headstrong, she would often disobey them. Let me put it this way—she was a girl who just wouldn't take no for an answer.

One day when she was supposed to be doing her homework, Goldilocks decided to go for a walk in the woods instead.

After a while, she came to an adorable little cottage. Everything about the house was so inviting—the little white picket fence, the flowers growing along the pathway to the door: tulips, pansies, even snapdragons—her favorite. Before you could say *Rumpelstiltskin*, Goldilocks was knocking on the door. No one answered. She pulled on the bell. Still no one answered. She tried the door. It was open. "Anyone home?" she shouted, and guess what? No one answered. Anyone else would have left, but not our Goldilocks.

As luck would have it, the cottage was home to Mr. and Mrs. Bear and their baby, Baby Bear. The Bears were married late in life by the wise old owl under the giant elm tree. Everyone came to the wedding: the rabbits, the birds (they provided the music,) the deer (ooh, they're so dear,) even Mr. and Mrs. Skunk (but they sat way in the back.) Now this particular morning, Mama Bear, who is very domestic and a Julia Child fan, had made a big pot of delicious…

Now this is a point of the story that is cloudy. She either made porridge, which is a hot cereal—very good with honey, and bears love honey—or else she made a delicious pot of hot soup (pasta e fagioli), made with macaroni and beans. Oh, bears love beans too! I've heard the story both ways—it for sure wasn't ham and eggs! If you ask me, it was pasta e fagioli, so let's go with the soup. O.K.? O.K.!

The soup was so hot when it came to the table that Papa Bear said, "Let's take a walk while this soup cools off." That's where the bears were when Goldilocks came to the door—get it? When Goldilocks walked into the house, she could smell something delicious. She tasted Papa Bear's soup. "Oh my," she cried, "this soup is too hot!" Then she slid over towards Mama Bear's soup. "Yuk, this soup is too cold," she shuddered. Then—you guessed it—she sampled Baby Bear's soup. "Yum yum," she said smilingly, "this soup is just right," and she ate it all up. You know, I wonder about that girl's manners—no one home, and she invites herself to lunch!

Now, anyone else might have left—but not our Goldilocks. She thought she'd have a little rest first. So, she sat down in Papa Bear's chair. "Oh dear," she moaned, "this chair is much too hard."

Then she scooted over to Mama Bear's chair, and it was soon clear it was much too soft. "This chair is much too soft," she said.

Then—you guessed it—she moved over to Baby Bear's chair, a gift he had just gotten from Auntie Bea Bear. Down she sat, and said, "This chair is just right." Then, guess what? Crash! I do believe that Goldilocks was big for her age, because this chair broke! I mean really broke—a leg went here, the seat went plop, a leg went there, the back went flop!

Goldilocks landed on the floor with a smack, and her backside hurt so much, she almost cried.

Now, you would think that once you have broken a chair you might slow down a bit, or think things over, or maybe leave—but not our Goldilocks. She gathered herself up and, before you could say *Jump! Jack! Jump!* she was upstairs lying on Papa Bear's bed. "Oh, no," she cried, "this bed is much too hard!"

Then she scooted over to Mama Bear's bed. "Oh, no,"
she moaned, as she sank, "this bed is much too soft."
Then—you guessed it—into Baby Bear's bed she climbed.
"Why, this bed is just right," she said, as she snuggled
under the covers. She placed her head on the pillow and
fell fast asleep. Let's face it, Goldilocks had had a
busy day and was ready for a nap.

In another part of the forest, Papa Bear looked at his watch and said, "Let's go home. The soup should be cool enough to eat by now." When they arrived, the first thing they noticed was that the door was open. "I'm positive I closed that door when we left," said Mama Bear. When they went inside, Papa Bear shouted, "Someone has been eating my soup!" "Oh," exclaimed Mama Bear, "someone has been eating my soup, too." "And look," cried Baby Bear, "someone has been eating my soup —and oh, no, it's all gone!"

Then, "Look, oh look," said Papa Bear, "someone has been sitting in my chair." I don't know for sure how he could tell, but they say that Mama Bear was very domestic, very neat, and an expert at fluffing pillows. "You're right, Papa Bear, and look! Someone has been sitting in my chair, too," said Mama Bear. Now Baby Bear was almost afraid to look and, sure enough, when he did, his worst fears were realized. "Someone has been sitting in my chair," he said, "and look, oh look, it's all broken." And Baby Bear started to cry real tears! Mama Bear comforted her Baby Bear.

"Shh, that someone may still be here," said Papa Bear, as he grabbed a tennis racket, and slowly started up the stairs. Mama Bear clung to Baby Bear as they followed behind.

"Look. Look," whispered Papa Bear. "My bed—someone has been sleeping in my bed." "Someone has been sleeping in my bed, too," answered Mama Bear. "Oh, wow, look!" hollered Baby Bear. "Someone has been sleeping in my bed, too—and she's still in it!"

Well, at that very moment, Goldilocks woke up, and was so
surprised to see the three bears looking down at her that she let
out a noise that startled everyone. Mama Bear, never known to be
a calm person, nearly dropped Baby Bear, which really frightened
Papa Bear, who tried to catch Baby Bear with the tennis racket,
scaring Goldilocks, and causing her to fall out of bed. Wowwee!

Everyone was running around and screaming and, for a while there, it was really a mess. But, by the time they worked their way downstairs and near the front door, things got calmer and a little clearer. Goldilocks apologized and Mama Bear invited her to lunch.

Fortunately, Mama Bear had made a big pot of soup, and before you could say *antidisestablishmentarianism*, Papa Bear had fixed Baby Bear's chair, and Goldilocks and the three bears sat down to a lovely lunch of soup and corn muffins with honey—and bears love honey as we know.

Goldilocks' mother was very concerned about her little girl and, boy, oh boy, was she relieved when Goldilocks finally came home! And the next time she told Goldilocks she couldn't go out until she did her homework, the little girl didn't even think about disobeying. Our Goldilocks had learned her lesson alright!

Sometimes, after her homework was done, Goldilocks would visit her new friends, the three bears. From time to time she would bring them homemade corn muffins. They would all sit down for a lovely lunch of soup and corn muffins, and have a good laugh about the interesting way they had met. Goldilocks would spread honey on the corn muffins. Oh, bears do love honey! And oh, the three bears did love Goldilocks!

GOLDILOCKS' PORRIDGE (OR FARINA)

INGREDIENTS	SERVES 1 (Goldilocks)	SERVES 2 (Goldilocks & 1 bear)	SERVES 4 (Goldilocks & 3 bears)
porridge or farina	2 tbsp.	4 tbsp.	8 tbsp.
water or milk	1 cup	2 cups	4 cups

DIRECTIONS

Heat water to boiling; milk to almost boiling. Add porridge or farina slowly, stirring constantly. Reduce to low heat. Cook 10 minutes or until thickened, stirring constantly. For thinner consistency, add more water and, for thicker consistency, cook a little longer. Serve with cold milk or honey…Bears love honey!

GOLDILOCKS' PASTA E FAGIOLI
(Macaroni and Beans)

- 2 tablespoons olive oil
- 2 garlic cloves, minced
- 1 cup water
- 1 8 oz. can tomato sauce
- 1 16 oz. can cannellini beans
- ½ pound elbow macaroni or ditalini
  fresh parsley, chopped
  grated cheese

DIRECTIONS

In a saucepan, fry the garlic gently in the oil until golden brown. Add the tomato sauce and water, and cook 10 minutes. Add the beans, stir gently, and continue to cook on simmer until beans are heated through.

Cook macaroni or ditalini al dente, drain, and add to bean mixture. Stir gently to combine. If it gets too thick, add a little more water. Add parsley to taste.

Serve immediately with grated cheese… Bears love cheese!

GOLDILOCKS' CORN MUFFINS

- 1 cup yellow cornmeal
- 1 cup all-purpose flour
- 1 8 oz. can of corn (drained)
- ½ cup sugar
- 2 teaspoons baking powder
- 1 cup (8 oz.) sour cream
- 2 eggs
- 6 tablespoons oil
  honey

DIRECTIONS

Preheat oven to 375°F. In a large bowl, combine the cornmeal, flour, corn, sugar, baking powder, sour cream, eggs and oil. Stir the ingredients to mix well. Divide the mixture evenly in generously greased muffin pans, filling cups almost to the top. Bake at 375° for 10 to 15 minutes, or until golden brown. Cool in pans on a wire rack for 5 minutes. Serve warm with honey…Bears love honey!